Cinderella Smith

by
Stephanie Barden

Illustrations by
Diane Goode

SCHOLASTIC INC.

ISBN 978-0-545-54147-3

12 11 10 9 8 7 6 5 4 3 2 1 13 14 15 16 17 18/0

Printed in the U.S.A. 40

First Scholastic printing, January 2013

Typography by Erin Fitzsimmons

To

Craig Virden, for fishing me out of the slush
Emma, Jack, Abby, Hannah, Isaac, and Will, for inspiration
And Tom and Joe, for everything
—S.B.

For Peter
—D.G.

1

A White Sneaker with Green Stripes

There was a very crazy knocking noise going on at my front door that I was pretending not to hear. Instead of going *knock-knock-knock* like most knocks, it went *knock-bounce-knock-bounce-knock*. And I wasn't even one bit wondering what was making that crazy noise because I already knew.

"Cinderella, can you answer the door, please?" my mom called.

I thought a little bit about that question. I *could* answer the door; I just didn't want to.

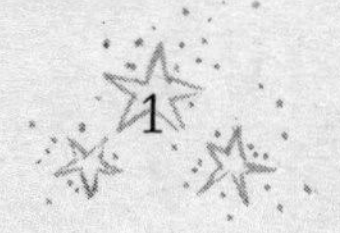

The bounce-knock-bouncer kept knocking.

"Cinderella!" my mom called. "Did you hear me?"

"I'm a little busy with something!" I called back, and that was true. I was lying on my bed looking through a coupon book full of back-to-school supplies and pretending I could get anything I wanted. Even the Puppy Power Messenger Bag. Even the Rock Star 40-Piece Value Pack.

"I'm busier finishing this page!" my mom yelled. And she wasn't talking about the page of a very, extremely exciting book. She was talking about a web page, because that's what she does for work. "Answer the door!" She said it very loud and stern, like she meant business. And in case you were wondering if she was a mean and bossy stepmom and that's how I got my name, the answer is no. She's just a regular kind of mom who is usually nice but kind of strict.

I rolled over to the edge of my bed and raced to the front door. So now you know that I didn't get my name from sleeping by an ashy fireplace in the kitchen like that other Cinderella.

"Finally!" said the bounce-knocker when I opened the door. "Think fast!" A white sneaker with green stripes flew toward me.

"Good catch, Tinder," said the bounce-knocker. The bounce-knocker, by the way, lives next door and is named Charlie Prince. He was making that crazy noise by dribbling his basketball and knocking on the door at the same time.

When we were very little, we called each other Tinder and Tarles because we couldn't say each other's name just right. As soon as I could, I started calling him Charlie; but he kept calling me Tinder because he knows it embarrasses me, and this is why. Back when I was calling him Tarles, I had, for some dumb reason, a crush on him. In this instance I am allowed to use the word *dumb* because it's about me and because it really was dumb. I used to walk over to his house every morning and ask him if he thought I looked pretty. If he said yes, I went back home and had breakfast. If he said no, I went home, changed my clothes, and tried again. And that is embarrassing stuff with a capital *E*.

"You don't need to put your name and address on shoes anymore," said Charlie. "No other kid loses just one shoe."

"You don't need to bring a basketball with you everywhere you go either," I said. I was a little bit proud of myself for coming up with that. Usually I never think of anything to say when he's pestering me.

Charlie shrugged his shoulders and kept dribbling. "Did you get your back-to-school letter?"

"Yep," I said.

"Who'd you get for a teacher?" he asked.

"Someone new named Mr. Harrison." I didn't want Charlie to know, but I was a little bit worried about getting a man for a teacher. I'd never had one before, and I didn't know what to expect.

"Oh no!" Charlie turned and jogged toward his driveway. "I got him too!"

"'Oh no' is right!" I said. Charlie and I haven't had the same teacher since Mrs. Adams in first grade.

All of a sudden I remembered my manners. "Thank you for my shoe!"

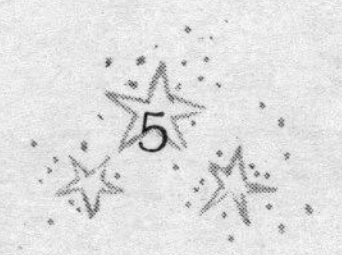

"No problem, Tinder!" he yelled back.

Then I was mad I'd remembered my manners after all.

"Who was at the door?" My mom looked down at the shoe in my hand and her eyebrow went up, which is not a good thing.

"Look at the bright side, Mom," I said. "I might have lost a shoe, but I got it back! And I'm almost one hundred percent sure this is the only one I lost all summer, except for the flip-flop at the beach. Dad said that one didn't count, though, remember? It was the lollapalooza wave's fault."

My mom's eyebrow stayed up, but Tess ran into the living room naked.

"Woilà!" she yelled. That's French for "ta-da!" and something I taught her. And, by the way, Tess is a nice little sister and not a mean step one, so that's not how I got my name either.

"Would you mind getting her ready so we can get your school things and tap shoes?" asked my mom. "If we have time we'll stop by the library too, so make sure we have all the books."

Keeping track of the library books is one of my chores, but I don't have a billion like the other Cinderella.

I helped Tess get dressed and then we searched for Mrs. C, a stuffed crocodile that has to go everywhere with her. Even though she's almost the most important toy in the world, she still gets lost a whole lot, and that causes a whole lot of problems. One time Mrs. C went missing for an entire day. When we finally found her, I super quick wrote on her tag *Property of Teresa Louise Smith* before she could get lost again.

While I was writing, I had a big *AHA!* which means a very, extremely good idea. I thought of something else that got lost a whole lot, and it wasn't car keys or the cordless phone. I ran to my closet, pulled out all of my shoes, and wrote on their bottoms:

If found please return to:
Cinderella Smith
410 Blackberry Lane
Seattle, Washington 98105

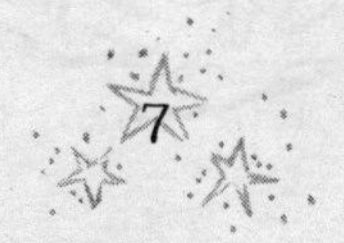

Some of the shoes were easy to write on, like my ballet slippers and new back-to-school silver sandals from Grandmother Smith, because they had smooth, flat bottoms. Some of the shoes were harder, like my rain boots and gym shoes. They had wavy and zigzagging bottoms, and I had to make the letters extra big and puffy. My old tap shoes—which I just grew out of, by the way—had black bottoms. I had to use nail polish on them because pens didn't work.

When my mom saw what I was doing, her eyebrow went way up high; and that is mostly a very bad sign, like I mentioned earlier. But then her eyebrow went back down. She said she

guessed it was okay and maybe even a good idea, after all. And ever since then I've been naming and addressing my shoes as soon as I get them to keep them safe.

So by now you've probably figured out how I got my name, which is just a nickname, for the record. My real name is Josephine-Kathryn with that little line thing in between. Everyone calls me Cinderella, though, on account of my trouble with losing shoes. *Alas. Alas* is something I say when I'm a little bit frustrated and a little bit sad. Since I like the sound of that word, especially if I say it all dramatic and sigh-y, it makes me feel a little bit better. And when you have shoe trouble as bad as I do, you end up saying *Alas* a lot. *Alas.*

2

Shiny, Ruby Red Tap Shoes

"Cinderella, phone for you," my mom called. "As soon as you hang up, we can leave."

I don't get a lot of phone calls, so this was pretty exciting news.

The voice on the phone said very loud and bossy: "Who did you get for your teacher?"

And I knew right away that it was Rosemary T., who lives just down the block and always talks like that.

"I have someone named Mr. Harrison," I said.

"So do I!" said Rosemary T. "Hannah and Abby do too, and so does Rosemary W."

Rosemary W. was the new kid last year. Since all of a sudden we had two Rosemarys in one class, we had to start adding the initial of their last name to tell them apart. At first Rosemary T. couldn't stand it, but by the end of the year she didn't mind because they were friends and even went to summer dance camp together.

"I've been calling everyone on my cell phone this morning to find out who their teacher is," said Rosemary T. "Emma and Amy and Nicole have Mrs. Kirk."

"That's too bad," I said. Emma and Amy and Nicole were in dance class with us, along with Rosemary W. and Hannah and Abby. Then I thought of something else. "You have a cell phone?"

"Yes," she said.

"Awesome!" I was very impressed.

"It's my sister Andrea's

old one. She's getting a new one for back-to-school, and she said I could use it. Guess what else?"

"What?" I asked.

"I'm getting my ears pierced!"

"Super awesome!" I said. I've wanted to get my ears pierced for forever, but my mom won't let me, and she doesn't want to talk about it anymore. If I ask about it even by accident, she adds another day to the time when I can finally get them done. *Alas.* Maybe my mom is a little wicked after all.

"Rosemary W.'s getting hers pierced," said Rosemary T. "Hannah already has hers and Abby might too."

"Wow," I said.

"You should get yours done," she said.

"I can't," I said.

"Why not?"

"My mom doesn't think I'm responsible enough yet."

"Maybe she would if you would quit losing shoes," said Rosemary T.

"Maybe," I said.

"Keep asking her all the time. That's what I did all summer long."

"I already tried—," I started to tell her, but she interrupted.

"And it's not that expensive, if that's the problem."

"I don't think it's—," I started to say, but she interrupted again.

"I've got to go. My mom is taking us to the mall for back-to-school shopping."

"We're going back-to-school shopping too," I said.

"Maybe I'll see you there." She hung up and didn't even say good-bye.

"Guess what, Mom?" I yelled. "Rosemary T. called me on a cell phone, and she's getting her ears pierced. She said Rosemary W. and maybe even Abby are, too."

"I see," said my mom.

"Do you think maybe, possibly, I could get mine too?" I asked.

My mom's eyebrow went up.

"You know what they say: the more the merrier!" That's something my Grandmother Smith always says. She

especially says it when I ask if I can do something she's doing, like reading Dear Abby or watching one of her soap operas.

My mom's eyebrow went up even higher.

"I take it back; I take it back!" I yelled. "You didn't hear that, right? Right?"

"Hear what?" said my mom.

"*Phew*." I wiped my forehead all dramatic.

When we got to the mall, it was very, extremely crowded with back-to-school shoppers.

My mom didn't want to lose us, so she held on to Tess with one hand and me with the other. The ear-piercing place was right in the middle of everything, and right there was Rosemary T. with her big sisters.

"Hi, Rosemary T.," I said.

She looked up from where she was studying all the earrings. "Hi." She looked very grown up, with a purse over her shoulder and shopping bags at her feet and no mom in sight.

"Where's your mom?" I asked.

"She having coffee and letting us shop by ourselves," said Rosemary T. Then she stared hard at my hand that was holding on to my mom's. I let go

of it quick, but I felt a little alone without it.

"Did you finally talk your mom into letting you get your ears pierced?" she asked.

"No." I thought I'd better change the subject super quick. "What did you buy?"

"So far I've gotten three shirts and a pair of jeans," she said, "but we just started."

"I'm on my way to get a new pair of tap shoes," I said.

"I got a new pair right before dance camp started," she said. "But I might get another new pair for class."

"I can't wait for it to start next week," I said.

"I can't either," said Rosemary T. "I wonder if Miss Akiyama will move me and Rosemary W. up a level. We got really good over the summer."

"Have you made a decision yet?" the ear-piercing lady asked Rosemary T.

"Yes. I want these." Rosemary T. pointed down to a pair.

"Go get your mom and we can get started," said the ear piercer.

"I'll just call her." Rosemary T. pulled a cell phone out of her purse.

"Rosemary!" Rosemary W. ran up to Rosemary T.

She had a purse slung over her shoulder and was with her big sister too.

"You got here just in time, Rosemary!" said Rosemary T. "I'm going to get these." She pointed to a pair of earrings in the glass case.

Rosemary W. and all the big sisters crowded around to see which pair she'd chosen.

"Hi, Rosemary W.," I said.

Rosemary W. looked up. "Oh, hi, Cinderella. Are you getting your ears pierced too?"

"She can't yet," said Rosemary T. "She's not grown up enough."

Tess grabbed my hand and pulled me and my mom toward a shop with plastic horses in the window. And I was not mad at her one little bit. I was glad to get pulled away.

"Bye," I called to the Rosemarys and their big sisters.

"I'm just asking out of sheer curiosity and no other reason," I said to my mom. "How much does it hurt to get your ears pierced?"

"They do it differently now," said my mom, "so I'm not sure. When I had mine done, I went to a doctor's office. He pinched my ears really hard until they were numb and then stuck big needles through."

"Wow," I said. "That must have hurt like the dickens."

"I didn't feel a thing," said my mom. "Your uncle was in the exam room with me, though, and he fainted."

"Because of all the blood and guts?" I asked.

My mom laughed. "There was no blood and guts. He was just a little squeamish."

We found everything on my school supply list at Office Mart. I didn't get a Puppy Power Messenger Bag because my old backpack was still fine, but I did get a box of sparkly pencils and scissors with pointy ends.

We just had to get mini cinnamon rolls because they smelled so good, then we went to the dance shop. A pair of the most beautiful tap shoes was in the window. They were shiny ruby red with a fancy bow, but were really spendy. I tried on a pair of regular black ones and my feet had gone up one whole size. The next pair fit perfectly, but when we went to the counter to buy them, my mom surprised me with a capital *S*. She asked if they had the red ones in my size, and she bought me those instead! I do not know why she did that, but maybe she's not so wicked after all.

3

Slippery-soled Silver Sandals

On the first day of school every year my dad takes the morning off from work and walks me to school with my mom and Tess. He says he likes to meet my new teacher and see my new room. That way when he thinks about me during the day, he knows how to picture things.

When we headed out the door, Tess grabbed my mom and dad by the hands so they could swing her through the air. I felt a little left out, so I grabbed on to my dad's other hand to be part of the chain, and we started walking.

When we got to the end of our block, we walked right by Rosemary T. and one of her sisters getting into their mom's car.

"Hello, Taylors," said my dad.

"Look!" Rosemary T. yelled through the closed window, pointing to her ears.

"They look great!" I yelled back.

Tess jumped up and down between my mom and dad trying to see Rosemary T.'s ears.

Rosemary T. looked at her and saw we were all holding hands. She whispered something to her big sister, and they both started giggling.

I thought about letting go of my dad's hand; but holding hands and walking to school together on the first day is something we always do, so who cares if they think it's funny?

"See you in class," I said, and our chain of Smiths kept walking to school.

For the first time ever on the first day of school, we climbed up the huge stairway to the second floor. Second-floor kids were running up and down the stairs, and it felt kind of good to be one of them, but kind of worryish too. My new silver sandals felt slippery, and I did not want to fall on those stairs with all those big kids around. I held on to the handrail supertight with a capital *T.*

We got to my new classroom almost late because of walking so slowly and swinging Tess through the air. I quick met my teacher, Mr. Harrison, and then let my parents talk to him while I went to find my seat. It turned out there were no name tags on the desks. Either big kids don't have them or Mr. Harrison doesn't know that having your own desk on the first day is a lot of help.

I looked around the room and saw that Rosemary T. and Hannah and Abby were already sitting together. They were at a table for four people, but Rosemary W. was sitting in the last spot. That was the spot they would have saved for me last year. Abby was using a cootie catcher to tell Rosemary T. her fortune. They were giggling and didn't notice me at all.

My feelings started hurting like the dickens.

I just stood in the middle of the room and didn't know what to do. My mom and dad left, and I just kept standing there.

Mr. Harrison said for us all to take a seat, which really just meant me because I was the only one still standing. I sat down super quick and stared right at the front of the room.

"Happy first day of school! I'm Mr. Harrison!" Our teacher bounced up and down a little on his toes. "Let's start with attendance so I can get to know all of you."

My name wasn't for a while, so I looked around the classroom. Mr. Harrison didn't have any books on his shelves or things hanging on the walls. Every name he called said "Here" until the person sitting next to me yelled "Present!" I jumped on account of the loud voice and the different word.

"That's a refreshing change of pace," said Mr. Harrison. "I was getting a little tired of only hearing 'Here's.'"

Everyone laughed, especially Logan Dalton. He was the person sitting next to me and the person who'd said "Present." Logan was in my class last year and was big into vocabulary words. I looked around my table for the first time and saw that I was sitting with the smart boys. That was a weird place for me to end up, but it could have been way worse.

If I had ended up with Charlie at the loud sports boys' table, he might have called me Tinder and thrown things at me and yelled "Think fast" all the time. Christopher Martin was across from me with his supplies out on his desk, ready to go. He had two rulers, maybe in case one broke in the middle of a math problem. Trevor Watson was across from me too and was already reading, because that's what he does. He had his book on his lap, so I couldn't tell what it was about.

"Erin Devlin?" said Mr. Harrison.

That was a name I'd never heard before.

"Here!" called a girl on the other side of the room. She had long, black hair with bangs straight across and was wearing a tie-dyed T-shirt.

"I believe we have something in common," said Mr. Harrison.

"We do?"

"Yes," said Mr. Harrison. "You're new here too, just like me. Where do you hail from?"

"Los Angeles," Erin, the new girl, said.

"Hoo-ray for Hollywood," said Mr. Harrison, except he sort of sang it.

"Have you ever seen a movie star?" asked Rosemary T. without raising her hand.

"Lots of times," said Erin.

"How about a Laker or a Dodger?" asked Jack from the loud sports boys' table.

"Only when I went to a game," said Erin.

"Awesome," said Jack.

"Very awesome," Mr. Harrison agreed.

He started back in on attendance and called Abby's name and then Hannah's. Both times I looked over at their table and we waved to each other.

"Josephine-Kathryn Smith?" said Mr. Harrison.

I started to raise my hand and answer, but Rosemary T. raised hers faster. I got very confused and pulled my hand back down.

Mr. Harrison said, "Josephine-Kathryn?" to Rosemary T.

"No," said Rosemary T. "My name is Rosemary Taylor, but nobody calls Josephine-Kathryn that name. She's called Cinderella."

Mr. Harrison laughed, and I was so surprised my mouth popped open. No one had ever laughed at my name before, except maybe Charlie. Then Rosemary T. laughed, and Rosemary W. laughed to be just like her. A few other people joined in. Now I was very, extremely confused. I'd never thought that my name was funny before.

"Are you trying to give the new guy a hard time?" asked Mr. Harrison.

"No, really, that's her name," Rosemary T. said.

"Truly?" asked Mr. Harrison. "A princess in our midst? Should I bow?"

Everyone laughed, and I shrank down in my chair.

"She's not a real princess," said Rosemary T., forgetting to raise her hand.

"She just has a lot in common with the real Cinderella," said Rosemary W.

"This sounds like a very interesting story," said Mr. Harrison.

"It's not really," said Rosemary T.

Kids started looking at me, and I shrank down a little bit more.

"But now I'm curious," said Mr. Harrison. "Someone fill me in! Once upon a time . . ."

Everyone laughed very loud and my cheeks got hot and I sank down more. Then all of a sudden I had had enough. I sat up very straight. "Excuse me!"

Mr. Harrison looked at me quite surprised.

"I think we should get back to attendance," I said. "Mrs. Bentley, the school secretary, does not like it when attendance gets to her late."

"I see," said Mr. Harrison. "Thank you for the heads-up."

"You're welcome," I said.

"And who are you?" he asked.

"I'm Josephine-Kathryn Smith," I said.

"Ah," he said, "the infamous Cinderella. Or do you prefer Josephine-Kathryn?"

I thought for a minute, wondering which I preferred.

"Cinderella has a nice ring to it," said Mr. Harrison. "And it's quite unique."

I nodded, but kept thinking. Maybe now that I was a big kid upstairs it was time for a more regular name.

"You'd likely never meet another Cinderella," he said. "Unlike the Rosemarys, for instance, that we have two of in our classroom alone."

I nodded again, but still wasn't sure. Maybe my nickname was funny. Maybe people would start laughing at me, like today.

"Who wants to be ordinary and have a name like everyone else?" he asked. "When you can be extra ordinary?"

That extra ordinary thing did it. "I'll stay being Cinderella," I said.

"Hoo-ray!" said Mr. Harrison. "I'm very glad. Now let's finish taking attendance before Mrs. Bentley fires me."

The class laughed and I did too, liking my name again and feeling a little bit not-ordinary.

4

Gladiator Sandals

When the bell for recess rang, everyone jumped out of their seats and lined up by the door. I had to be super careful on the stairs again on account of my slippery shoes and all the big kids racing to get outside. I started sliding over to the four-square game that the Rosemarys had started, trying to scuff up my soles even more.

"Cinderella! Cinderella!" my neighbor Louie called from the kindergarten play area.

I slid over to the fence that keeps the little kids safe from the big kids. "How's school so far?"

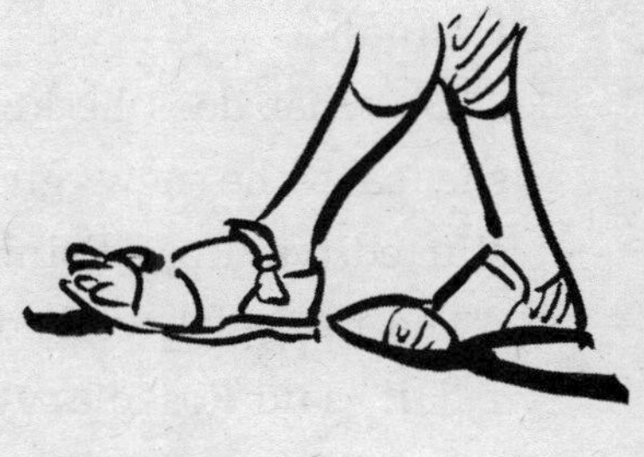

"It's great!" he yelled. "See you later, alligator."

"Bye for now, dairy cow!" I yelled back.

I slid over to the four-square game where Hannah and Abby had joined the Rosemarys.

"What are you doing, Cinderella?" Rosemary T. stared at my sliding feet.

"I'm getting my shoes less slippery," I said. "Can I play?"

"Wouldn't you rather play with the kindergartners?" asked Rosemary T.

"I bet they'd all slide around the playground with you," said Rosemary W.

The two of them giggled. I stopped sliding.

"What do you guys think about the new teacher?" Abby asked.

"He's annoying," said Rosemary T.

"He thinks he's sooooo funny," said Rosemary W., "and he's not."

"He sure likes your name, Cinderella," said Hannah.

"So what does he know?" Rosemary T. said. Then she saw the new girl across the playground and started waving. "Erin! Over here, Erin!"

The new girl walked toward us slowly.

"Hi!" said Rosemary T. "Do you want to play four-square?"

"Maybe," she said.

"I love your gladiator sandals," said Rosemary T.

"Thanks," said Erin.

"Did you get those around here or back home in Hollywood?" asked Rosemary T.

"Back home."

"Too bad," said Rosemary T. "I would love to have shoes like that."

"Do you have pierced ears?" Rosemary W. asked.

"Yes," said Erin.

"So do I!" Rosemary W. tucked her hair behind her ears so the red sparkly stones showed.

"Me too." Rosemary T. turned her head right and left so her blue ones twinkled.

"I like your earrings," Abby told the Rosemarys.

"We both got our birthstones," said Rosemary W.

"I like yours too, Erin," said Hannah.

"Those are awesome," said Rosemary T. "I'll get some like that when I can change mine."

I looked over at Erin's ears. She was wearing dangly peace signs. "I have a T-shirt kind of like your earrings," I said.

"You do?" She stared at me very serious. I got a little nervous thinking maybe she didn't like the idea that I had something the same as her.

"Take Hannah's square." Rosemary T. bounced the ball to Erin.

Erin let the ball bounce by her. "No thanks." She looked at me very serious again.

"Cinderella, right?"

I swallowed. "Yes."

"I need to talk to you," she said.

"Okay." Now I really was worried about my earring comment, which didn't seem bad to me at all the more I thought about it.

Everyone looked at Erin. She didn't say anything for a minute. "In private."

I kind of gulped a little bit again. "Okay."

She started walking away from us, toward the benches by the basketball nets. I followed after her, and we both sat down.

"Are you for some reason mad that I have a T-shirt like your earrings?" I asked.

"Why would I be mad about that?" she asked.

"I don't know," I said. "It just seemed like maybe you were."

"I don't care about my earrings," she said.

"I would if I had earrings," I said. "But probably mainly because I can't have any yet."

"Why not?" she asked.

"It's a long story," I said.

"Once upon a time?" Erin smiled.

I smiled back. "So what did you want to talk about in private?" I felt a little more brave now that

I knew she wasn't mad at me.

She looked at me very serious again, and I got back to being worried.

"I need advice," she said.

"I've never been the new kid before," I said.

"I have, tons of times," she said. "I don't need advice on that."

"Oh," I said. Then I got very, extremely excited, because I was just dying to give some advice. My favorite TV show is *It's Me or the Dog,* which stars Victoria, who is always giving people advice about their dogs. I also like it when me and my Grandmother Smith read Dear Abby letters from the newspaper. We try to figure out what we would tell the person before we see what Abby has to say. But before I could find out more, the bell rang and recess was over.

By the time lunch finally came I could barely wait to talk to Erin. When we were washing our hands, Rosemary T. told Erin that she should sit with us at lunch, which was pretty nice. Rosemary T. isn't the best at including everybody. It might mean I'd have to wait a little longer to hear about the advice Erin needed, but maybe she wasn't feeling so private about it anymore. She might talk about it in front of other people now.

The line for milk moved very slow. When I finally headed to our table, there was a chair saved for me next to Rosemary T. At least I thought it was saved for me, but when I got there Rosemary T. said: "Sorry, Cinderella. We promised to save a place for Erin."

"Oh. Okay." I walked over to the other table. "Is this seat saved?" I asked Hilary. We were best friends in kindergarten, but we hadn't been in the same classroom since.

"No," she said. "Go ahead."

"Thanks." I sat down and tried to listen to Hilary and Katie talk about a video with two dogs and a cat in it. Usually I would have loved to hear all about it, but my insides were hurting like the dickens, so much that I couldn't pay attention. The lunchroom was noisy, but even though I was in the middle of a super crowded table and a super crowded room, I felt alone. I chewed and tried to swallow and blink-blink-blinked my eyes. There was no way I was going to

cry right then and there. No way with a capital *N*.

"Erin! Erin!" Rosemary T. yelled, and waved to her. Erin had just made it through the lunch line. She headed over to Rosemary T.'s table and was about to sit down; but then she looked around, saw where I was sitting, and headed over.

She sat right down next to me and didn't ask if any places were saved or anything.

The alone feeling started to go away, and I could swallow again.

"What's for lunch?" I hardly ever got to buy lunch, so I was very interested.

"Cheese pizza and pears and green beans," she said.

"Yum and yum and yuck," I said.

"What?" she asked, and then she got it. "Oh yeah. Yum and yum and yuck."

"So what do you need advice on?" I whispered, in case she was still feeling private.

"On wicked stepsisters," she whispered back.

"Hmm," I said, very surprised.

"You know about them, right," she whispered, "because of your name."

"Hmm," I said one more time.

"Because I'm about to get two of them, and I really need some expert help."

I knew I should tell her that I didn't know anything about wicked stepsisters and that I really got my name because of my shoe trouble. The thing was, I didn't want her to get up and go sit with the Rosemarys or anywhere else. I also really liked the idea of giving someone advice, like I mentioned before. I just sat there and thought and thought. I guess I thought a little bit too long though, because Erin got tired of waiting.

"If you don't want to help me, just say so," she said.

That kind of woke me up. "I want to help you," I said.

"Good," she said very loud and final, and there was no getting out of it now.

5

High-heeled Shoes with Curlicue Toes

Me and Tess and my mom walked home from school with Louie and his mom and little sister. Louie loved kindergarten and talked a mile a minute about pizza for lunch and the classroom pet turtle. I had a lot on my mind, so I didn't talk at all. I was thinking about advice giving and wicked stepsisters and what Dear Abby would have to say on this subject.

After we left the Thomases at their house on the corner, my mom said, "A penny for your thoughts."

That doesn't really mean she's going to pay me anything, though. It's just a way to get me started talking.

"There's a new girl in my class named Erin Devlin," I said.

"What's she like?" asked my mom.

"She's really tall and has long, dark hair and bangs and pierced ears," I said. "And I'm just mentioning her ears to explain her and not for any other reason."

"Got it," said my mom.

"I'm sitting at the smart boys' table," I said.

"You are?" asked my mom.

"There were no places left with Hannah and Abby and the Rosemarys."

We walked in the house, and it just smelled regular—not like chocolate chip cookies. *Alas.*

"I have some sort of homework to do today," I said. "It involves watching *It's Me or the Dog.*"

My mom's eyebrow went up just a little tiny bit like she didn't quite believe me.

"The new girl, Erin Devlin, and me are doing a research project on our own," I said. "Can I have my snack in front of the TV?"

"You can if you keep an eye on Tess for me," said

my mom. "I've got to get the website to my client today."

"Okay," I said, putting some crackers and apple slices on a plate.

Tess and I sat on the floor in front of the TV.

"This is sort of homework, sort of research," I told Tess. "The new girl is going to get some wicked stepsisters, and she needs advice on how to handle the situation."

Tess nodded. She sat Mrs. C on the floor between us.

"So I want to watch Victoria very, extremely closely and get some advice-giving tips from her. Then I need to learn as much as I can about wicked stepsisters."

I took a bite of apple and thought of something. "I better take notes." I ran to get a spiral notebook from the extra school supplies in my room. I grabbed one for Tess too.

When *It's Me or the Dog* started, I wrote across the front of the notebook:

WICKED STEPSISTERS NOTEBOOK.

Tess looked over at my notebook and started scribbling on the cover of hers.

In this episode there was a family with a little

hot-dog dog called Wickersham. He was a smidgy little dog, but he barked at everyone. I couldn't just watch Wickersham, though, even though he was funny, because I needed to study Victoria.

The first thing she did was ask a whole lot of questions, like how old Wickersham was. Then she said to pretend she wasn't there and sat in a corner just watching the people and the dog. In hardly any time Victoria knew how to fix the problem. She got Wickersham to stop barking; and by the end of the show, the whole family was happy.

Before I forgot anything I grabbed up my notebook and turned to page one. On the first line I wrote:

ADVICE GIVING all in capitals.

On the next line I wrote: *Ask lots of questions. Pretend to be invisible. Watch close.*

Tess was scribbling in her book too. "Woilà!" She held up a picture.

"Good," I said. "Now we need to learn about wicked stepsisters."

I pulled *The Big Book of Fairy Tales* off the bookshelf. I sat down next to Tess and started reading "Cinderella."

"*Once upon a time there was a little girl whose dear mother died.*" I looked at Tess to make sure she wasn't too shook up by this news, but she wasn't.

"Her father married for his second wife the proudest and unkindest woman that ever was seen." Now why would a dad marry someone like that? He has a kid, for heaven's sake; you'd think he would be very, extremely careful who he brought home. That makes me wonder why Erin isn't worried about a wicked stepmother too. That should be my first question for her.

I wrote *QUESTIONS:* really big at the top of the next page in the notebook and then:

1) *What about a wicked stepmother?*

I kept reading. "*She had two daughters who were exactly like her in every way.*"

Tess pointed to a picture of the wicked stepmother and her daughters arriving at Cinderella's house.

The stepsisters had brought tons of chests that were all piled up on top of the carriage. Frilly clothes and sparkly jewels and high-heeled shoes with curlicue toes were all spilling out.

"Messy," Tess said.

"Yes, sir." I wrote on the *QUESTIONS* page:

2) *Are they messy?*

3) *Do they have lots of luggage?*

We kept reading and I kept adding to my list of questions: *Are they loud and bossy? Are they lazy and sleep a ton? Do they stare in the mirror a lot? Do they have lots of clothes? Do they have big feet?*

"I think that's a pretty good list of wicked stepsister questions," I said when we got to the end of the story.

"More," said Tess.

"More questions?" I asked.

"More reading," said Tess.

I sighed a big sigh, but I'm not sure why because I like reading fairy tales and I like Tess too, most of the time.

6
Flip-flops

"What about your wicked stepmother?" I asked Erin the minute we got our first recess the next morning.

"What wicked stepmother?" she asked.

"The one that comes with the wicked stepsisters," I said.

"They come with a stepfather."

"Is he wicked?"

"He's okay, I guess," she said.

I followed Erin over to a bench and showed her

my notebook.

"What's that?" she asked.

"A *WICKED STEPSISTERS NOTEBOOK,*" I said.

"Where did you get it?"

"I made it." I fished the pencil out from the metal spirals and opened to the first page. "I have some questions for you."

"Okay," she said.

"What can you tell me about your wicked stepsisters?"

"Not much," she said. "I haven't met them yet."

"Why not?" I asked.

"I'm not going to meet them until right before the wedding."

"That seems a little fishy."

"It does?" she asked.

"Yes," I said. "Maybe your stepfather is very, extremely ashamed of them."

"Maybe," said Erin. "But I think it's just because they're away at college."

"Hmm," I said, "so they're a lot older and bigger than you."

"I guess so," she said. "What are your stepsisters like?"

My heart dropped a little bit inside me. "I actually don't have any."

Erin stared hard at me.

"That's not why I'm called Cinderella," I said, and then got all nervous about what would happen next.

"So you can't help," she said.

"Yes, I can," I said. "Even though I don't have stepsisters, I can still help you find out if yours are wicked or not."

"Of course they're wicked," said Erin.

"But you haven't met them yet, so how do you know?" I asked.

"Because all stepsisters are wicked," she said.

"No, they're not," I said very sure, even though I wasn't so sure really.

Her forehead crinkled into one big frown and she opened her mouth to say something, but Rosemary T. appeared right by the bench just then.

"What are you two doing?" she asked. She didn't say it like it was a question, though.

"We're . . . ," I started to answer.

"None of your business," Erin said.

That made Rosemary T.'s eyes go all big and round.

She thinks every-
thing is her business.
She looked like she didn't know what to do and so she just huffed off.

I was a little bit shocked by all this and just sat there for a minute. "Wow," I finally said.

"Why 'wow'?" asked Erin.

"'Wow' because you just talked to Rosemary T. like that. I wish I could sometimes."

"Why can't you?" she asked.

"I'm not sure." I thought hard about why not, but I couldn't figure it out right then.

Erin's forehead was still crinkled in a big frown. I started to worry that Erin didn't want my advice and help after all now that she knew I wasn't an expert. Maybe she wouldn't sit by me at lunch either. Maybe she would sit with Rosemary T. even if wicked stepsisters weren't any of Rosemary T.'s business.

I was about to say "A penny for your thoughts" when the bell rang for the end of recess and we started to line up.

Charlie got in line right behind me. He bounced his basketball as close to my feet as he could.

"Quiet in the line, everyone!" called Mr. Harrison. "Let's try to set a good example."

I wanted to slip my foot under one of Charlie's bounces and send his basketball across the playground, but two things stopped me. One, I wouldn't be setting a good example. And two, I was wearing my flip-flops, and the ball might smash my toes.

Mr. Harrison told us to take out our math journals. He pointed to the blackboard and bounced a little bit on his toes.

"This math problem has three parts," he said. "Part A is to write it down in your math journals. Part B is to figure out the answer. And part C is to write about the Process."

People's hands went up all over the room.

"I don't get the Process part," said Jack.

A lot of other people didn't get it either.

"Just give it a try," said Mr. Harrison, "and we'll discuss it in a minute."

So I did. I wrote down the problem in my math journal, which was:

A. The chocolate cupcake is not taller than the vanilla cupcake. The strawberry cupcake is shorter than the chocolate cupcake. Which cupcake is the shortest?

Next I wrote the answer, which was:

B. The strawberry cupcake.

Then I wrote about the Process, which was:

C. These cupcakes must have been homemade and not store-bought since they're different sizes. I'm glad strawberry was the shortest, because that is my least favorite.

"As soon as everyone's finished at your table," said Mr. Harrison, "have a discussion."

"Did everyone get strawberry as the answer for *B*?" asked Logan.

"Yep," we all agreed.

"What did you write for *C*?" Trevor asked.

"I didn't write anything," said Christopher, "because I didn't know the right answer."

"I didn't write anything either," said Logan. "What did you write, Cinderella?"

"I wrote that these cupcakes must have been homemade and that strawberry is my least favorite flavor, so it was good it was the shortest."

"That can't be the right answer," said Christopher.

"I don't think there is a right answer," I said. "It's journal writing, for heaven's sake."

"There has to be a right answer," said Trevor, "because it's math."

"Okay," said Mr. Harrison. "Who would like to share?"

Logan raised his hand.

"Yes, Logan?"

"Our table wants to know what the right answer is," said Logan.

"What do you think it is?" asked Mr. Harrison.

Rosemary T. raised her hand. "Strawberry," she said.

"We know *that* answer," said Logan. "We mean the answer to *C*, the Process part."

"What do you think it is?" Mr. Harrison asked again.

"I am flummoxed," said Logan, trying out a new vocabulary word.

"What did you write down?" Mr. Harrison asked.

"I didn't write anything," said Logan.

"You didn't explain Process," said Trevor, "so we didn't know the right answer."

"I see." Mr. Harrison stopped bouncing. "I was hoping you would try to figure out what the Process was on your own. Who can tell me what the word *process* means?"

A few people raised their hands, and Mr. Harrison called on Charlie. "The way you figure something out," Charlie said.

"Exactly!" Mr. Harrison's excitement started coming back. "The Process is just the way you organize a problem so you can solve it, especially a complicated problem with a lot of information. For instance, you could have made a chart with the three flavors of cupcakes across the top." Mr. Harrison started drawing on the blackboard. "And under each flavor you could write what you know about it."

Logan raised his hand. "So what's the right answer for *C*?"

"There is no right answer," said Mr. Harrison. "Everyone's Process is different." Everyone groaned a little, but I kind of liked the idea of no right answers all the time.

I spent the rest of the morning only half thinking about school things and half thinking about Erin and her stepsisters. Every time I looked over at her she had that same frown on her face. I didn't know if it was because we were writing in our science journals or because of her stepsisters problem. Figuring out if they were wicked or not would be complicated. There were a lot of questions that needed to be answered and a lot of facts to gather. Then, all of a sudden, I had a big, huge *AHA!* which, by accident, I said out loud.

Charlie laughed, and all the loud sports boys joined in.

"Did you have a breakthrough, Cinderella?" Mr. Harrison asked.

"As a matter of fact, I did," I said.

"Do you want to share?" he asked.

"Not with everyone." I looked over at Erin and smiled. Her frown went away and she smiled back. Then I just couldn't wait for lunch, because I knew that Erin would want to sit with me and not the Rosemarys after all.

We sat at a table with horse girls and artsy girls. The Rosemarys were far away at the other table. Every time I looked over at them they were staring at us and whispering.

"I think Rosemary T. is still surprised that you told her to mind her own business," I said.

"Really?" asked Erin.

"Yep," I said. "Every time I look over at the Rosemarys they're staring at us and whispering."

Erin looked over at the Rosemarys. Sure enough, they were doing it. Erin leaned over to my ear and put her hand up to her mouth. "I like lunch today," she whispered.

I laughed because I was so surprised by her saying that. I leaned over to her. "Is liking chicken tenders and pineapple a secret?"

"No," she whispered back. "I'm just trying to bug the Rosemarys."

"Oh," I said. I glanced over at the Rosemarys and

saw that they kept staring. "I think it's working. By the way, I have a great idea about that thing we were talking about at first recess."

We finished eating, headed outside, and sat on one of the benches.

"Solving the problem of your possibly wicked stepsisters is complicated," I said.

"I agree," said Erin.

"We need a Process," I said.

Erin looked interested.

"There will be a lot of information, so I'm going to make three pages."

Erin scooted closer to me on the bench so she had a good view of the notebook.

"This page is for NOT-WICKED THINGS." I wrote that big across the top and turned the page. "This is for POSSIBLY WICKED THINGS." I turned the page again. This is for FOR-SURE WICKED THINGS."

"Great," said Erin.

"So, ready for some questions?" I asked.

"Yes!" she said.

"Do your possibly wicked stepsisters have big feet?" I asked.

"Maybe," she said.

I turned to the POSSIBLY WICKED page and wrote: *Maybe big feet.*

"Are they messy?"

"I don't know."

"Are they loud and bossy?"

"I don't know," said Erin.

"Are they lazy?" I asked.

"I'm not sure," she said.

"Do they stare in the mirror all the time?"

"I told you; I haven't met them yet!" She sounded a little frustrated.

"Maybe I should talk to someone who knows them better," I said. "Like your stepfather or your mom."

"Okay," she said.

"Let's have a playdate so we can figure this all out," I said.

"Great!" she said.

"It can't be today though, because my mom likes some warning," I said. "And it can't be tomorrow, because I have my first dance class of the year."

"Oh," said Erin, and she sounded sad.

"Do you like to dance?" I asked. "Maybe you could sign up for it too. Lots of girls from our class are in it."

"I usually play soccer in the fall," said Erin, "but I can ask my mom."

"You should," I said. "Because the more the merrier!"

7

Tap Shoes with Clip-on Orange Bows

I was very, extremely excited Thursday for the first dance class of the year. I carpool with Rosemary T. since we're neighbors, and that used to be fine and dandy; but this year it's a little bit of an *Alas*.

"Mrs. Smith," said Rosemary T. "My mom brought home the leftover brownies you brought to the PTA meeting. They were delicious."

"I'm glad you liked them," said my mom.

"My mom asked if she could have the recipe," said Rosemary T.

"Of course," said my mom. "I'll email it to her."

Rosemary T. and my mom talked on and on about cooking. I was only half listening, though, because my mind was on dance class.

"It's been a long time since I've danced," I said. "I hope I didn't forget everything."

"You should have gone to dance camp this summer with me and Rosemary W.," said Rosemary T.

I shrugged my shoulders and acted like I didn't care, but I did.

"We learned a whole bunch of new steps," said Rosemary T. "And when dance camp was over, we practiced a lot. If you're way behind, I could give you some private lessons."

I couldn't think of anything worse than that, but my mom said, "That's a nice offer. Thank you, Rosemary."

Luckily we pulled up to the dance studio right then so I didn't have to say thank you too. *Phew!*

I remembered pretty much everything though, even with the summer in between. I put my shoulders back and walked around in my ballet slippers with my toes pointed all through our warm-up.

When we changed into our tap shoes, I remembered even better. I step-ball-changed and step-ball-changed like there was no tomorrow. And that just means I was having fun, fun, fun.

After we danced for a while, Miss Akiyama, our dance teacher, sat us down to have a serious talk about the Autumn Recital. She said our class would be doing two dances. One dance was called the Pumpkin Prowl, and the other was called Pumpkin Blossoms.

Rosemary T. just couldn't wait to tell her mom all about it on the drive home. She talked a blue streak, which means very fast without stopping.

"The Pumpkin Blossoms dance has a solo part," she said. "One person gets to be the Pumpkin Blossom Fairy and wear a special tutu and a crown and clip-on orange bows on her tap shoes. Rosemary W. thinks I would make the best Pumpkin Blossom Fairy in the whole class."

"I'm sure you would do a fine job," said Mrs. Taylor.

"Miss Akiyama said we could invite anyone we wanted," said Rosemary T. "Let's invite everyone we know. Maybe I'll make special invitations on the computer."

"People would like that," said Mrs. Taylor. "Who will you invite, Cinderella?"

"I will for sure invite my mom and my dad and Tess," I said, "and also my grandmothers. I might even invite the new girl, Erin. Usually I wouldn't invite a kid, but she's thinking about taking dance class, so she can see what it's all about."

"I was going to invite Erin," said Rosemary T. "I was going to send her one of my special invitations."

"Go ahead," I said.

"But getting two invitations is dumb," said Rosemary T.

"Why?" I asked.

"Because it just is," said Rosemary T.

We pulled up in front of my house.

"Mom, do you think it's a good idea if the person who gets the solo part gets to invite Erin?"

"That seems fair," said Mrs. Taylor.

Rosemary T. crossed her arms and smiled like she'd just won. I climbed out of the car feeling like I'd lost, but then I had an *AHA!* Miss Akiyama hadn't picked a Pumpkin Blossom Fairy yet. I had as much chance of getting picked as

Rosemary T., even if I didn't go to summer dance camp.

"Thank you for the ride," I said to Mrs. Taylor. And "It's a deal," I said to Rosemary T.

8

White Mary Janes with Little Heels

It turns out that when you move you get very busy going to new doctors and dentists and orthodontists. Finally Erin had a free afternoon, and we got to schedule a playdate. While we waited for her mom to pick us up after school, she told me we had to be a little sly about her possibly wicked stepsisters.

"My mom is tired of answering questions about them," she said.

"I know all about moms getting sick and tired of

talking about things," I said. "We have two subjects that are strictly off-limits at our house: getting a dog and getting my ears pierced."

"There's my mom," said Erin when a periwinkle blue Beetle bug car pulled up to the curb.

"You must be Cinderella," her mom said.

"Yep." I held out my hand.

She reached her hand right out the window, and I gave it a good shake, with a good grip, like my dad showed me. Nobody likes a limp-noodle hand.

"This is a very cute car," I said, making polite conversation.

"Thank you," said Mrs. Devlin.

"It's also in my favorite color," I said.

"It's in my favorite color too," said Mrs. Devlin. "The girls will be wearing periwinkle blue dresses in the wedding."

"Cool!" I said. "I wish I could see them."

"You can," said Mrs. Devlin. "The dresses arrived last week."

"I tried mine on right away," said Erin.

"And she looked very cute," said Mrs. Devlin. "Now we just have to hope that Anna and Julia will look as good."

My ears perked up because I figured I knew who

Anna and Julia were. I also figured, since Mrs. Devlin started it, I could ask a few questions. I pulled the *WICKED STEPSISTERS NOTEBOOK* out of my backpack. "Who are Anna and Julia?"

"They're Erin's soon-to-be stepsisters," said Mrs. Devlin.

"Those are nice names," I said.

"They are," said Mrs. Devlin, but then she didn't say any more.

"I have a sister," I said, trying to stick to the subject at hand. "Her name is Tess."

"That's a nice name too," said Mrs. Devlin.

"If she was a boy she was going to be named Chester," I said. "That always makes me think of *The Cricket in Times Square*. And that cricket could be very loud sometimes, like sisters," I said.

Mrs. Devlin laughed.

I waited a second, but she didn't say anything else. I wrote *Maybe loud* on the POSSIBLY WICKED page.

"Here we are," said Mrs. Devlin.

We jumped out of the car, and she opened up the trunk to get the groceries.

"Your car even has a cute trunk," I said.

"It's small," she said. "We'll have to use a bigger

car to pick people up from the airport."

"I see," I said.

"I bet you girls would like a snack," she said. "Why don't you show Cinderella your room, and I'll call you when it's ready."

I followed Erin upstairs. There were different stripes of color on one wall and boxes everywhere. "I'm still unpacking," she said, "and picking out a paint color."

"I wish I could change my room color. It's still light yellow from when I was a baby." I plopped down on her mattress, which was right on the floor, and kicked off my shoes. I opened my notebook. I wrote *Maybe lots of luggage* before I forgot.

She plopped down next to me. "What did you write?"

"I wrote 'Maybe lots of luggage' on the POSSIBLY WICKED page," I said. "They might be bringing a ton on account of needing a bigger car to pick them up from the airport.

"Luggage is wicked?" she asked.

"Not regular amounts of luggage, but loads of it are," I said. "Also, your mom didn't say if they're loud or not, so that means they could be."

"I guess they could," she said.

"So that goes on the POSSIBLY WICKED page."

Erin scrunched her eyebrows together and got all quiet.

"What's up?" I'd figured out that scrunched eyebrows meant she was thinking hard.

"I'm kind of loud," she said.

"Me too!" I said kind of loud. Then I got a big idea and so I said a big *AHA!*

"'*AHA!*' what?" she asked.

"*AHA!* You're going to be a stepsister too!" I said. "We should put you in this notebook."

She scrunched her eyes almost closed and smiled. "Let's start."

I wrote on the FOR-SURE WICKED page: *Erin=Kind of loud.*

"Snack's ready!" Mrs. Devlin called.

"BE RIGHT THERE!" Erin yelled at the top of her lungs.

A big bowl of popcorn and glasses of lemonade were waiting on the counter for us.

I tossed a kernel up in the air and caught it in my mouth. "My record is eight in a row. I want to beat the world record, but I'm not sure what it is."

Erin tossed a kernel up, but it hit her chin. "I'm terrible at this." She tossed another one up, and it bounced off her cheek.

When the fifth one landed on the floor, Mrs. Devlin said "Erin" very serious.

"If you have a rule about no playing with food," I said, "I started it."

"It's not a rule," said Mrs. Devlin. "I just don't like to waste too many."

"You don't have the law of three seconds here?" I asked.

"What's the law of three seconds?" asked Erin.

"Scientists studied how fast things that fall on the ground pick up germs," I said. "If you pick up food before three seconds, it's just fine to eat it."

"I'll have to think about that one," said Mrs. Devlin. "Are you going to show Cinderella your dress?"

"Sure!" We ran back upstairs to Erin's room.

Erin opened her closet. There were so many clothes on so many hangers that everything was all squashed together.

"Your closet is packed full to bursting!" I said.

"I collect T-shirts," said Erin. "They're my favorite thing to wear, but I was afraid it would be too rainy and cold to wear them now."

"Everyone thinks that about Seattle," I said. "But it's nice in the fall at least until Halloween. Then it starts to rain."

"Do you get wet when you trick-or-treat?" asked Erin.

"Sometimes." I looked through her T-shirts. *"AHA!"* I said.

"'*AHA!*' what?" Erin asked.

"You have lots of clothes." I picked up the *WICKED STEPSISTERS NOTEBOOK* and wrote *Erin=Lots of clothes* on the FOR-SURE WICKED page.

"I have an *AHA!* too!" said Erin. "I'm lazy. Look

at all this stuff I still have to unpack!"

"'*AHA!*' is right!" I wrote: *Erin=Lazy* on the FOR-SURE WICKED page.

"Here's my dress for the wedding." She pulled the periwinkle dress out of the closet. It was long and slippery soft and shiny.

"It's very pretty," I said.

"I guess so," said Erin. "I don't really like dresses, though, and this goes all the way to the floor. These are the shoes." They were white Mary Janes with little heels. "I have to be careful not to trip. Want to see Anna's and Julia's?"

"Definitely," I said.

"Follow me," said Erin. "They're in the guest room."

I followed Erin to the room next door carrying the *WICKED STEP-SISTERS NOTEBOOK*. "The first thing is that the closet is very big," I said. "So writing 'Maybe lots of luggage' on their POSSIBLY WICKED page was probably right."

"When I went to Disneyland

last year, my mom and I were going to share a suitcase," said Erin. "We had too much stuff, though, so we each had to bring our own."

"Good remembering." I wrote: *Erin=Lots of luggage* on the FOR-SURE WICKED page. "The next thing is that that is a very big mirror on that closet door. That probably means they like to stare at themselves a ton." I wrote: *Mirror-starers* on the stepsisters' POSSIBLY WICKED page. "Do you look at yourself a lot?" I asked.

"I'm not sure," she said.

"I have been lately," I said, "because I'm trying to learn to raise one of my eyebrows at a time like my mom."

We both stared in the mirror and made weird faces at each other.

"Cinderella, your mom's here!" called Mrs. Devlin.

"I'll be right there," I called back. "Start paying attention to if you look in the mirror a lot."

"Okay," said Erin.

We headed out of the guest room to the stairs.

"Don't forget your shoes," said Erin.

"Oops," I said. "Thanks."

9 Thumbtacked Sneaker

The next time I packed up my ballet bag I ran into trouble of epic proportions. That means something hugely terrible happened, and this is what it was: one of my new tap shoes was missing. I looked everywhere and all over our house in a very sly and sneaky way. I did not want anyone to know what was going on, especially my mom. Finally, when I was searching through Tess's room for the third time, I decided to tell my little sister. I thought I would explode if I didn't tell someone.

"I can't find one of my tap shoes anywhere," I whispered.

She didn't look impressed by this news because she's used to me losing shoes.

"Remember the Autumn Recital I told you about?" I said. "And the solo part? If I don't have my tap shoe, I might not get to be in it."

Tess handed me Mrs. C.

I sat down next to her on her big-girl bed and dangled my feet over the bar that keeps her from rolling off. My stomach went all grumbling and nervous. Everyone was tired of me losing shoes. Miss Akiyama and my mom and dad would be mad-mad-mad. Rosemary T. would probably get picked for the Pumpkin Blossom Fairy and get to invite Erin to the recital. My eyes started to water, but I did not want to cry. I jumped off Tess's bed and started tap dancing to get all the bad feelings out.

"Why tapping?" asked Tess.

"I don't know; it just seemed like a good idea," I said. "I had some bad feelings stuck inside me, and now they're going away. Do you want to tap too? The more the merrier!"

Tess climbed off her bed and started tap dancing with me.

"I just thought of something." I stopped tapping and was a little out of breath.

Tess stopped too.

"Maybe I left my tap shoe at dance class." The hurt in my stomach went almost all away. "I must have! But just in case, I'm going to pack my sneaker with the thumbtack stuck in it. It makes a pretty good tap shoe too."

And it was good that I had packed my thumb-tacked sneaker, because I didn't find my tap shoe at the dance studio either. It wasn't in the dressing room or the waiting room or in the Lost and Found. *Alas.* I wondered what Miss Akiyama would say, but I didn't have too much time to think on that because dance class started.

First we warmed up, which involves holding on to a barre and doing pliés and relevés.

Those words are French for bending your knees and going up on your toes, and we always do this part in ballet slippers because you can't go up on your toes in tap shoes. Next we practiced the Pumpkin Blossoms dance. I was hoping Miss Akiyama would be so impressed with my dancing that she wouldn't notice my feet at all, but she did right away. *Alas* again.

"What do you have on your feet, Cinderella?" she asked.

"One regular tap shoe and one homemade one." I hoped that would be the end of the discussion.

Rosemary T. rolled her eyes at me and made a big face to Rosemary W. "That is so dumb," she said.

"And weird too," said Rosemary W.

"Please explain." Miss Akiyama sounded more interested than mad.

"My tap shoe is missing," I said. "So I brought my thumbtacked sneaker to practice in."

Rosemary T. rolled her eyes again.

Miss Akiyama looked at me quite serious. "I would rather you practice in ballet slippers today and find your real tap shoe before our next class."

"Okay," I said, even though I didn't know how I was going to find it.

That night Erin called me to say that she'd spent so many minutes staring at herself in the bathroom mirror that her mom had to knock on the door to make sure she was okay. Her name was all over the FOR-SURE WICKED page.

"I wish you were in my dance class," I said, getting ready to tell her about my shoe.

"My mom decided I can only do soccer this fall," said Erin. "With the wedding coming up, we have a lot going on. I can start in the winter if I want to, but I have to choose that or basketball."

"I'm always having to choose too," I said. "My mom is big into not overscheduling." Then I whispered, "Actually, if I don't find my tap shoe, maybe I'll play basketball too."

"You lost your tap shoe?" Erin asked.

"Yep," I whispered, not wanting my mom to hear, "and I can't find it anywhere."

"I'll help you find it," said Erin. "That's what friends are for."

That made me feel so happy that I stopped worrying about my missing shoe for a while. But by the next morning it was all I could think about.

It was a little drizzly, and me and Erin shared

my umbrella while we waited for school to start.

"I thought you said it wouldn't rain until Halloween," said Erin.

"This isn't rain," I said. "This is dribbly-spit."

"Dribbly-spit?"

"That's what we call it at my house," I said. "I'm not sure what the scientific name is."

The bell rang and we lined up.

Charlie and Jack bounced their basketballs in figure eights around us and the Rosemarys, who were sharing an umbrella behind us. The Rosemarys squealed every time the boys got too close, but we pretended not to notice.

"Not even the rain, I mean dribbly-spit, stops them," whispered Erin.

We checked the Lost and Found at recess. It was huge and covered three lunch tables.

"If we don't find my tap shoe in here," I said,

"maybe we could make 'Lost' posters for it like they do for missing pets."

"That's a great idea," said Erin. "We can hang them all over. Yuck!" She dropped someone's head-gear back into the pile.

On account of how careful we were looking, we knocked some things off the tables. We picked them back up, though; and that's when the school secretary, Mrs. Bentley, saw us. She thanked us a ton for helping clean up the mess instead of being at recess. And I didn't think until later that she probably didn't know we made the mess in the first place.

When Mrs. Bentley walked us out to the playground, I told her the whole story of my lost tap shoe and the recital and the posters me and Erin were going to make. She told us we could hang three on the doors at school so everyone who came in the building would see them.

When recess was over and we got back in to class, I had an *AHA!* and raised my hand.

"Yes, Cinderella," said Mr. Harrison.

"Can I make an announcement, please?"

"Certainly!" said Mr. Harrison, very enthusiastic as usual.

I stood up. "I have lost a very important tap shoe.

1 2 3

It's shiny, ruby red with a fancy bow, and has my name on it. If anybody finds it I would be very, extremely grateful. Also, there will be a reward." I hadn't thought about the reward thing until that very minute. I added it because the class was looking a little bored. People put their hands up. "Can I take questions?"

"Sure," said Mr. Harrison.

"What's the reward?" asked Charlie.

"It's a surprise-prize, which is the best kind." But really I didn't know what it was yet.

"Will you give yourself a surprise-prize if you find your own shoe?" Logan asked.

"Of course," I said.

Rosemary T. raised her hand. "Miss Akiyama won't let you be in the recital if you don't find your shoe," she said.

"That's not a question," I said. "And I'm not doing comments now."

"Time for PE, everyone!" said Mr. Harrison.

I heard some groaning from the Rosemarys' table, and that made me smile. I like PE pretty well, but I like it even better knowing that the Rosemarys don't.

10

Autographed Orange High-tops

Walking home from school with my mom and Tess and Erin should have been very, extremely fun, but I was too nervous. Erin and I were going to make posters for my shoe, and that meant I had to tell my mom the news. I took a big breath of air to get brave and spilled the beans.

"Mother," I said.

"Mother?" My mom's eyebrow started to go up.

"I have some bad news to share, and it is bad with

a capital *B*. My tap shoe is missing."

My mom's eyebrow kept going up.

"But, but, but," I said, trying to make her eyebrow go down again. "Erin and I are going to make posters all about it today and hang them all over the block."

Her eyebrow stayed half up and half down.

"We already checked all through the Lost and Found and I made an announcement and Mrs. Bentley says we can hang posters at school. Also, I searched all over the house and I told Miss Akiyama and I searched all over the dance studio too."

I looked at my mom, but I couldn't tell which way her eyebrow was going.

"Halt!" said Tess. That's army for "stop," and she said it because we were standing in front of our house.

Erin and I raced inside and up to my room so we wouldn't have to talk any more about it.

"Do you have a shoe collection?" Erin asked.

I looked around my room. "I didn't think I did, but maybe I do."

"Why is this one in a frame?" she asked.

"I guess because it's sort of special," I said. "It's half of the first pair of shoes I ever wore. They were a present, but I lost one on the way home from the hospital."

"It sure is cute," said Erin. "What's this one doing on a shelf?"

It was an autograph-covered orange high-top.

"I lost it down the bleachers at a basketball game," I said. "The team signed it before they sent it back to me."

"That's pretty awesome," she said.

"Snacks ready!" my mom called. "And the poster supplies are laid out."

Erin and I ran to the dining room and got to work. We wrote *LOST* across the top of each poster in big letters. Next we drew a picture of my tap shoe. We made it ruby red with a fancy bow like in real life. We wrote my shoe size and then we put down my name and address. At the very bottom we wrote *REWARD* really big to get

people's attention, since it worked in class.

We headed out the door with some tape and heard the bouncing noise.

"There's Charlie playing basketball of course, like I told you he would be," I said. "And I guarantee you that Rosemary T. will appear as soon as she sees us."

"*Alas,*" said Erin.

And all of a sudden there was Rosemary T.

"Hi, Erin," she called, racing out of her house. "What are you doing with Cinderella?"

It was pretty obvious what we were doing, so I just went ahead and told her. "We're putting up posters about my missing tap shoe on all the streetlights."

"You're not allowed to put one up on our streetlight," she said.

"Why not?" I asked.

"Because you didn't ask permission."

I thought about ignoring Rosemary T. and just taping one up. Then I thought she'd probably tear it down as soon as we left.

Right then Mr. Taylor drove up in his shiny car. "Hello, girls," he said.

"Hi, Daddy!" said Rosemary T. "This is the new girl I told you about, Erin. Erin, this is my dad who is in charge of a bank."

"Pleased to meet you, Erin," said Mr. Taylor. "Good to see you as always, Cinderella."

"Good to see you too." Right then I got a big *AHA!* "Mr. Taylor, would it be okay with you if we taped one of our posters up to your streetlight?"

"It's not my streetlight," he said. "It's the city's."

"Are we supposed to ask the city if we can put these up?" I got a little bit nervous because I am usually a very law-abiding citizen.

"Oh no," said Mr. Taylor. "They don't care as long as you take them down afterward."

"I promise we will as soon as we find my tap shoe," I said.

"Then tape away," he said back.

There was only one other person on my block who cared about the posters, and that one other person was Charlie. Of course. I wanted to put a poster on his light post too, though, so we'd just have to put up with him.

"Hey, Tinder and Erin," he called.

"Tinder?" asked Erin.

"It's a long story that I will tell you about later," I said. Charlie never called me that at school, which I realized was really pretty nice.

"Can we put one of our posters up here?"

"Sure," he said, and bounced his ball over to the streetlight to read the poster.

"You didn't need to include your name and address, you know," he said. "If anyone ever finds a missing shoe, they know who it belongs to."

I tried to put a "you're very annoying" look on my face.

He laughed and dribbled his basketball away. Just then the top part of the poster came untaped and folded down. I jumped up to try to get it taped again, but it's very hard to jump in clogs. I kicked them off and tried again. Erin jumped too, but she couldn't reach either.

"Do you need help?" Charlie yelled from his driveway.

"No!" I yelled back, even though a taller person would have helped.

Then Erin had the brilliant idea to pick me up and boost me. She got me high enough so I could reach it and then we crumbled to the ground. All we could hear was Charlie laughing. I was very, extremely embarrassed, and Erin probably was too. We gathered up the tape and two leftover posters and my shoes to head home, but there was a problem.

"Where's my other clog?" I asked.

Erin twirled around in a circle, spying all around. "I don't see it anywhere."

I looked over to Charlie and yelled: "Did you take my shoe?"

"What would I do with a dumb old girl's shoe?" he yelled back.

I couldn't think of anything to say back to that, so I had to go home without one shoe. *Alas.*

During dinner, our neighbor Mr. Hansen came over, looking grumpy and embarrassed.

He was carrying his dog in his arms, and his dog was carrying my clog in his mouth.

"He won't drop it," Mr. Hansen said. "I don't want to yank it out because it might ruin your shoe."

"Ralph?" I said, all shocked. "You stole my shoe?"

Ralph started wriggling, looking very cute and a little bit naughty.

"You're not going anywhere until you give up the shoe," said Mr. Hansen.

"How about a trade, Ralph?" I held up a bread-stick. "Can he have some?"

"It's fine by me," said Mr. Hansen.

I walked over to Ralph and waved a piece of bread-stick under his nose. He started drooling down my clog.

"Mmm," I said, taking a big bite.

That did the trick; he dropped my shoe and grabbed the breadstick. "Thanks, Ralph."

"This dog will be the end of me." Mr. Hansen said that all the time, and I believed him.

"Did Ralph get out today?" I asked.

"Not that I noticed," he said, "but he must have at some point, unless you threw your shoe into our yard."

"Nope," I said. "So now he knows how to break out and break back in again," I said.

"I guess so." Mr. Hansen took a cup of coffee from my dad.

"Hey, Mr. Hansen," I said. "Did Ralph happen to find a ruby red tap shoe too?"

"I don't think so," said Mr. Hansen.

"Could you check around when you get home?" I asked. "It's a very important shoe. Rosemary T. said I can't be in the dance recital without it."

"That is an important shoe," said Mr. Hansen.

"And if I can't be in the recital, Rosemary T. will for sure get to do the solo part."

"I see," said Mr. Hansen.

"She told me that at recess today," I said. "She said she is the best dancer in the class and she's also Miss Akiyama's favorite. I'm not sure about all that, though."

"That's enough, Cinderella," said my mom.

"I am not spreading rumors, it's . . ."

My mom's eyebrow started to go up, and the room got very quiet.

My cheeks went a little warm. "By the way, Mr. Hansen, there's a reward for my shoe."

"Rewards are good," said Mr. Hansen. "What are you offering?"

"I'm not sure yet," I said.

Mr. Hansen smiled. I started to feel a little better about almost getting in trouble in front of him.

"We'll keep our eyes open," he said. "Mrs. Hansen, me, and especially Ralph."

11

Black, Patent Leather Tap Shoes

At my next dance class I still had not found my tap shoe. *Alas.* I told Miss Akiyama about all the searching and posters, and she just stood there and looked very, extremely stern. Finally, after tons of seconds, she said something.

"Keep practicing in your ballet slippers for now, but I want you to find that shoe!"

"Aye, aye, Cap'n," I said, which we say around my house when we get an order. "I mean, yes, Miss Akiyama."

"Girls," Miss Akiyama said to everyone. "Now that we've learned all the parts in the Pumpkin Blossoms dance I'd like to have you start taking turns being the fairy."

Rosemary T. raised her hand. "Will we get to wear the special tutu, crown, and shoe bows?"

"Not yet," said Miss Akiyama. "You will get to practice with the wand, however."

"Awesome," the class said.

Rosemary T. raised her hand again.

"Just a minute, Rosemary T.," said Miss Akiyama. "Cinderella, why don't you go first?"

I was so happy, I wanted to start tap dancing up a storm right then and there. A few of the girls looked disappointed, though, so I didn't. Rosemary T. pulled her hand down and looked mad, but Abby gave me a bump and Hannah smiled.

Miss Akiyama handed me a gold wand with a star on the end. I waved it around a couple times to get used to it, then stood where the Pumpkin Blossom Fairy is supposed to stand. The piano player, who I think might be Miss Akiyama's mother, started playing. I did the five taps with my right foot, which is how the dance starts, and then began.

Rosemary T. did not turn into a Dancing Pumpkin

when I tapped her on the head. She told Miss Akiyama that she didn't know when it was her turn because she couldn't hear me tapping up to her without my tap shoes. The next time I tapped her on the head a little harder, which she had kind of asked for.

"Ouch!" Rosemary T. yelled, and the piano player stopped.

"Pumpkins do not talk," I said. "Even magic ones."

"You make a terrible Pumpkin Blossom Fairy!" she said.

"Well, you make a terr . . . ," I started to say; but I saw Miss Akiyama looking more very, extremely sterner than usual. I bit my tongue for real, but not too hard.

"Let's have the next person try," said Miss Akiyama. "How about you, Hannah?"

I handed Hannah the wand, and she took her turn trying out the dance. Next Abby went; then Rosemary T.; then Rosemary W.; then Emma, Nicole, and Amy.

"Good work, girls," said Miss Akiyama as class finished up.

Dance class was regular and normal the next week until the end when Miss Akiyama said she had an announcement. She said she had picked who the Pumpkin Blossom Fairy would be, and that person was me!

I just couldn't believe that I got picked for the solo part. I was sure it would be Rosemary T., because she always gets picked and my tap shoe was still missing. Rosemary T. just couldn't believe it either. She crossed her arms and stomped out of dance class very loud in her black, patent leather tap shoes.

On the whole car ride home her mom kept asking her if she was feeling okay and she kept saying she was, but I knew that wasn't the truth. I kept all quiet because I did not want to be the one to tell Mrs. Taylor that her daughter had not gotten the solo part. When we finally got to my house, I super quick jumped out of that car and raced inside.

"I have some very, extremely exciting news!" I yelled. "With a humongous capital *E*!"

Tess came running into the room waving her hands over her head, just like you should when someone yells about very, extreme excitement. My mom walked into the room slowly with her eyebrow way up. I knew her eyebrow was up on account of me not using an inside voice, but I just couldn't help it.

"I would like to introduce to you the PUMPKIN BLOSSOM FAIRY!" I yelled, and did a big, low curtsy.

"Congratulations!" said my mom.

And we all three danced in the hallway together in a kind of made-up tap dance way.

After that I called my grandmothers to invite them. My Grandma B. said yes right away. She lives very close, and we can pretty much always count on her coming to things like spelling bees and lemonade stands. My Grandmother Smith said yes too. She can be tricky, because she lives a little bit far away and has to take a train. She said her friend's granddaughter just got the lead in her school play, and now she herself would have something to brag about.

Next I called Erin. When I told her about being the Pumpkin Blossom Fairy, she yelled so loud that I had to pull the phone away from my ear. Then she yelled, "Take that, Rosemary T.!"

"Oh yeah, that reminds me," I said. "Would you maybe like to come to the recital? Then you can see what dance class is all about."

"I would love to come to the recital," she said. "Thank you very much for the invitation."

12

Big, Old, Brown, Ratty Tap Shoes

"Now is this real rain or just dribbly-spit?" Erin pulled her chair up next to me because we were inside for rainy-day recess.

"This is the real deal," I said.

"I thought so." She handed me an envelope. "I have an invitation for you too."

The envelope was really big and thick, and I couldn't wait to open it, because I love getting mail. Inside the first envelope was another envelope, which was sort of weird; but I like opening envelopes, so who cares. Inside the second envelope was a fancy-looking card with curlicue letters. What the fancy letters said was that I was cordially invited to Erin's mom's wedding!

"Do you think you can come?" she asked.

"I'll have to ask my mom for sure, but I bet yes!" I said.

"I'm also supposed to ask you if you can come early and keep me company," said Erin.

"The wedding doesn't start until five, and my mom says everyone will be running around like crazy getting the house ready."

"Don't you mean getting themselves ready?" I asked.

"That too," said Erin. "But also the house. They're getting married right there."

"That's handy," I said.

"Sort of," said Erin. "But it means we have to finish unpacking and hang pictures. I also have to choose my paint color."

"I was getting used to the stripes," I said.

"I was too," said Erin. She lowered her voice. "Another reason you need to come over early is because my almost-stepsisters are arriving that morning."

"That's perfect," I said. "Then we can watch them and figure out if they're wicked or not before the wedding."

"When we figure it out," said Erin, "what will we do?"

Rosemary T. appeared right then. "What's that?" She pointed to my wedding invitation.

In our house we have a rule that everyone has to be invited to everything so no feelings get hurt. I wasn't sure what to say.

"It's an invitation," said Erin. "I'm inviting Cinderella to my mom's wedding."

Rosemary T. got a weird look and stormed away. I felt a little bit bad about that, but I couldn't think about it for too long because Erin asked me that question again.

"So when we figure out about my stepsisters, what will we do?"

I thought for a minute and then I had a big *AHA!* I remembered something about weddings. "If they're not wicked, we won't do anything. If they are wicked, we can stop the wedding."

"We can?" Erin looked very, extremely surprised.

"Yes!" I said.

Erin smiled the biggest smile I'd ever seen.

"I've seen it happen on my Grandmother Smith's soap operas," I said. "There's a part during the wedding when the minister asks the guests if they have any objections. If we think your stepsisters are wicked, then we'll just let the minister know and he'll have to stop it!"

"Really?" Erin kept smiling.

"Yep, but we'll have to pay close attention. We can't miss that part, because if you don't object right then and there, you have to forever hold your peace. That means you can never talk about it ever again."

"I'll be standing right up front," said Erin. "I'll make sure not to miss it."

"Perfect!" And everything was perfect until the fishy things started to happen.

The first fishy thing was that Rosemary T. made an announcement.

She walked up to the front of the room and sort of cleared her throat like she was very important. "I just want to tell everyone that you don't need to look for Cinderella's tap shoe anymore. I have an old pair that she can borrow."

Charlie raised his hand. "How do you know they'll fit? Maybe your feet are tons bigger than Cinderella's."

"They'll fit," said Rosemary T., and her cheeks turned a little pink.

"How old are they?" asked Logan. "Are they falling apart?"

"They aren't that old," said Rosemary T. Her cheeks got a little pinker.

"What color are they?" one of the girls who love horses asked.

"They're brown," said Rosemary T.

"Well, I think this is mighty nice of you," said Mr. Harrison. "Do you have anything to say, Cinderella?"

"This is all brand-new news to me," I said.

"Is there anything else?" he asked.

I knew what Mr. Harrison was hinting at, but this was Rosemary T. we're talking about.

"I'm speechless" was all I could come up with.

And I didn't get sent to the hall, and I don't know how to explain this except that maybe Mr. Harrison doesn't know about doing that yet.

The second fishy thing was during last recess. Erin and I caught the Rosemarys taking down our posters from the doors and squishing them all up. We got very, extremely mad and started yelling at them to stop. They told us that the posters didn't matter anymore on account of the shoes Rosemary T. was loaning me. We said that wasn't the point at all, but it was too late.

The posters were all so crumpled that they were ruined.

When my mom and Tess picked me up in the car to run errands after school, I told them I had two very important subjects to discuss.

"Subject number one is Erin's mom's wedding. Erin invited me!"

"That's wonderful," said my mom. "When is it?"

"Saturday, November first, at five in the evening; but Erin wants me to come over early. Can I go? PLEASE!"

"Of course," said my mom. "Where is it?"

"It's right at Erin's house," I said.

"Sara must be overwhelmed," said my mom. And Sara, by the way, is Mrs. Devlin's first name. "I can't imagine moving into a new house and planning a wedding at the same time."

"Erin has to finally finish unpacking and pick a paint color," I said. "She's sort of overwhelmed too."

"The wedding's the day after Halloween," said my mom. "Do you know what Erin's plans are for trick-or-treating?"

"We've talked about costumes," I said. "But not trick-or-treating."

"What do you think about inviting Erin over on Halloween to spend the night?" asked my mom. "That might be more fun for her and help her mom out a bit."

"I love that idea!" I said.

"Me too!" said Tess. She was a big fan of Erin's because Erin picked her up and twirled her around all the time.

"I'll call Sara and see what she thinks," said my mom.

"Awesome," I said. Then I remembered the fishiness.

I told her all about Rosemary T. saying I could borrow her big, old, brown tap shoes and the Rosemarys tearing down and destroying the posters.

"It doesn't sound fishy," said my mom. "It sounds like Rosemary T. is trying to be nice."

"Rosemary T. and 'nice' do not go together," I said.

"Now it seems like you're the one who's not being nice," said my mom.

"ME?" I said.

"You haven't spent much time with Rosemary this year," said my mom. "Maybe she's hoping that by loaning you her shoes, you'll be close friends again."

"Mother," I said. "You do not know Rosemary T. very well anymore." I was all full of disappointment in her.

We turned onto our block and something fishy was going on right there. The Lost Shoe poster on the Thomases' streetlight was missing. The one on the Hansens' was missing too. The one on Rosemary T.'s was missing, but no surprise there. All of the posters were gone except for the one on Charlie's, who was playing basketball in his driveway. Of course.

"Argh!" I yelled.

The car swerved and my mom yelled, "How many times do I have to tell you not to yell when I'm driving?"

I guess she'll still have to tell me a few more times, but I didn't say that out loud.

Instead I said, "Now do you believe me about the fishy business?"

"How do you know it was Rosemary T. who took down your posters?" my mom asked.

"Mother," I said, all full of disappointment all over again.

As soon as my mom parked, I jumped out of the car and went to see if Charlie knew anything about the fishy business.

"Hey, Tinder," he said.

"Do you know anything about my missing posters?" I asked.

He stopped dribbling. "The posters about your missing shoe are missing now?"

"As a matter of fact, they are," I said. "Except for the one in front of your house."

"That's because I wouldn't let Rosemary T. take it down when she tried," he said.

"Really?" I asked.

"Yep. She said again about you borrowing her big,

old, brown, ratty tap shoes and not needing your shoe anymore," he said. "But it's your poster, and it's my streetlight, so I told her to leave it alone." Charlie started dribbling again and moving his feet all over the place. "I mean, you still need to find your shoe, right? You don't want to wear Rosemary T.'s old shoes forever."

"Finally," I said, "someone besides Erin who gets it!" And I was feeling so good about Charlie right then that I almost wanted to say sorry for thinking he had ever stolen my clog.

13

Puppy Tooth-marked Clog

"It isn't raining today!" Erin ran across the playground Halloween morning to meet me.

"I know!" I said. "We won't end up being drowned-rat rock stars after all!"

We gave each other high tens and grinned at our costumes. We both had our hair pulled up in ponytails and were wearing black lipstick and nail polish. I was borrowing one of her rock-and-roll T-shirts. She was borrowing a tennis racket for a guitar.

We lined up to go inside, and the loud sports boys ran up, dribbling their basketballs. They were wearing long, baggy shorts and big tank tops with numbers on them.

"Are those your costumes or your uniforms?" I asked.

"They're both," said Charlie.

"Aren't you freezing?" asked Erin.

"Nah," said Charlie.

Two pumpkins, who were really Hannah and Abby, walked over to us holding hands.

"Our ballet recital sure made Halloween costumes easy this year," said Abby.

The Rosemarys were ahead of us in line.

"Are the Rosemarys princesses or fairies?" I asked.

"They're Good Witches," said Hannah. "Like Glinda from *The Wizard of Oz.*"

Mr. Harrison walked over to us wearing a referee uniform.

"Hey, Mr. Harrison," said Jack. "Are you a ref in real life?"

But I couldn't hear the answer because it was a crazy madhouse inside the school.

Pirates and cheerleaders and vampires and firefighters were everywhere.

During recess Erin told me that she was so nervous to meet her stepsisters that she couldn't even get excited about the Halloween party after lunch.

"Oh no," I said. "That is nervous."

She jumped up from the bench we were sitting on and started walking around it in circles.

"I know they're going to be wicked," she said.

"But we have a lot of information that maybe they're not." I opened up the *WICKED STEPSISTERS NOTEBOOK.*

Erin kept circling.

"There's nothing on their FOR-SURE WICKED page at all. And there are only four things, four little, tiny things on their POSSIBLY WICKED page: 'Maybe big feet,' 'Maybe loud,' 'Maybe lots of luggage,' and 'Maybe mirror-starers.'"

"What about things we don't have anywhere in the notebook yet," said Erin. "Things like loud and lazy and bossy and mean?"

"That's okay," I said, "because we have a plan, remember? If they are wicked—and that's not for sure at all—we'll just stop the wedding."

Erin plopped back down on the bench. "Oh yeah." She started jiggling her legs so much that the bench was wobbling.

"You're still nervous," I said. "Nervous with a capital *N*."

"I'm not sure if I'm nervous about them being wicked anymore," said Erin. "Maybe I'm just nervous about the whole thing."

"What whole thing?" I asked.

"The whole everything," she said.

At first I wasn't sure what she meant, and then I had a big *AHA!* "You mean that you're getting a new dad and new sisters and a whole new family?"

"Yes," she said.

"That's a lot of newness." I bounced up and down on the jiggling bench. "You also have a new house and a new school and new kids to get to know."

"Sometimes it feels like too much new," said Erin. She stopped jiggling but started blinking super quick.

I hated that feeling Erin was having. I hated trying not to cry.

"Hey, do you want to tap-dance?" I asked.

"What?" asked Erin.

"Tap dance," I said. "Sometimes tap dancing makes me feel better."

"I'm not sure," said Erin.

"This is the Pumpkin Blossom Fairy dance." I jumped up off the bench and tapped my puppy tooth-marked clog in front of me five times. Next I did some shuffles and ball changes and brushes and strikes and finished with a cramp-roll. "Ta-da!"

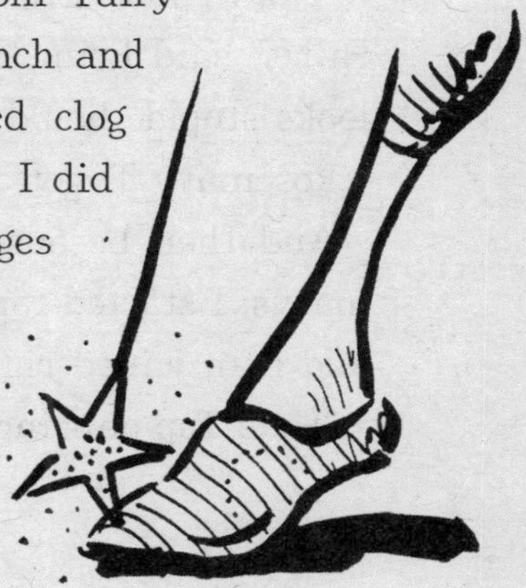

Erin didn't look sad or mad or nervous anymore. She was smiling.

"If you think watching makes you feel better, wait until you try it yourself!" I pulled her up off the bench.

I started tapping and shuffling and ball changing. Erin tried right along with me.

"What are you doing?" asked Rosemary T., appearing out of nowhere.

"What does it look like we're doing?" I said.

Rosemary W. was right there with her. "Why are you TAP DANCING on the PLAYGROUND?"

"Why not?" I did a few shuffles to the side.

"Because you look stupid," said Rosemary T.

I was a little bit shocked at her saying that. *Stupid* is a very, extremely mean and off-limits word in my house.

"No wonder Cinderella is the Pumpkin Blossom Fairy," said Erin. "No one who thinks tap dancing looks stupid should have a solo."

Rosemary T. got all shocked looking at that.

And then because I knew it bothered the Rosemarys, I started tap dancing right in front of them, and Erin joined right in.

"Hey! Tap dancing!" Abby and Hannah ran over to

us in their pumpkin costumes. "Can we do it too?"

"Sure!" I yelled. "The more the merrier!" And we all tapped together. The Rosemarys just looked at us for a couple seconds and then race-walked away as fast as they could, because they hate to run.

14
Wedges

My mom drove us over to Erin's the next morning. The house was all full of people delivering things and decorating. My mom went to find Erin's mom, and we stood out of the way on the stairs. I felt a little like Victoria from *It's Me or the Dog,* pretending to be invisible and watching closely.

"Which ones are your stepsisters?" I asked.

"I don't know," said Erin.

My mom appeared with Mrs. Devlin. She gave us

each a hug. "Today's the big day."

"Yep," said Erin. They hugged each other again.

"Jay will be here any minute with his daughters," said Mrs. Devlin. "I know it's a bit silly, but I'm going up to my bedroom to get ready and hide."

"Are you scared?" I asked.

"A little nervous," said Mrs. Devlin, "but that's not why I'm hiding."

"I'll get the girls all ready before I leave," said my mom.

"Thank you for everything," said Mrs. Devlin.

"Of course," said my mom. "We're so happy for you."

Mrs. Devlin smiled. "After you're ready, girls, why don't you find Anna and Julia and introduce yourselves." A car door slammed. "That's them now."

Erin's eyes got really big, and she grabbed my hand.

"I'll see you soon!" Mrs. Devlin raced up the stairs.

We followed her and went into Erin's room. My mom helped us into our dresses and French braided our hair. Noises came from the room next door.

"You two look lovely," said my mom. She took lots of pictures of us and then gave us hugs. "Be good. Have fun. I'll see you later tonight."

"What should we do?" asked Erin.

The room next door was quiet. "I guess go find them," I said.

Erin covered her mouth with her hands, and her eyes got all big again.

"As long as we're upstairs," I said, "maybe we should see how much luggage they have."

Erin nodded.

We tiptoed out of Erin's room and peeked into the room next door. It looked like an explosion had gone off, with books and clothes and bags everywhere.

"Oh dear," I whispered, "with a capital *O* and *D*."

Erin just stared.

We slipped into the room for a closer look.

"Wicked stepsisters are messy," said Erin.

We sat down on one of the beds, but first had to push some things out of the way.

I opened up the *WICKED STEPSISTERS NOTEBOOK* to the POSSIBLY WICKED page and erased *Maybe lots of luggage.* I turned to the FOR-SURE WICKED page and wrote*: Lots of luggage; lots of clothes; messy.*

Erin sighed.

"Let's go find them and get more information," I said.

The kitchen was crazy-busy. No one noticed when we came in and climbed onto the stools at the counter. Someone was rearranging the refrigerator to make room for the food that was being delivered. Someone was unpacking glasses from a box, and someone else was washing them. Flowers were being arranged in vases, and tablecloths were being ironed.

"I hope the one who's yelling about how full the refrigerator is isn't one of them," I said.

"Me too," said Erin.

"Or the one who keeps telling people where things

go," I said. "She seems pretty bossy."

"Yeah," said Erin.

"Everyone's busy in here," I said. "Whoever your stepsisters are, they're working hard."

"Except those two," said Erin, pointing to the kitchen table.

Two girls were just sitting there, looking sort of bored. One of them was talking on her cell phone, and the other one was texting on hers.

Erin and I looked at each other.

"What should I do?" she asked.

"I guess go introduce yourself," I said.

"I can't!" said Erin, all panicky.

"I'll do it for you." I slid off my stool and walked over to the table.

"Hello, I'm Erin's friend Cinderella." I reached out my hand to shake.

The girls just stared at me like I was from Mars or something.

"You know, Mrs. Devlin's daughter? The person you're going to be sisters with?"

The girls started cackling, but maybe it was more of a laugh.

"We're the caterer's daughters," one said. "We're just waiting for her to take us home."

"Oh!" I said, all relieved. I raced back to Erin. "They're not your stepsisters!"

"Phew!" said Erin.

"So that means that two of the busy people in here are!" I opened up the notebook to the NOT WICKED page and wrote: *Not lazy.*

The box unpacker set down a glass, walked over to the counter, and sat down with us.

"I recognize you from pictures my dad showed me," she said. "You're Erin."

Erin stared at her.

"I'm Julia, your big sister, almost."

Erin stared some more.

Julia smiled. "And that girl washing dishes is Anna, your other big sis."

Erin stared at the girl at the sink.

"Hi." I held out my hand. "I'm Erin's friend Cinderella."

Julia shook my hand. "That's an awesome name. Awesome nail color too."

I looked down at my nails. They were still painted black from Halloween. "Erin has the same color."

Erin looked down at her hands. Anna looked up from the sink.

"Hey, Anna," Julia called. "This is our almost-little sis, Erin, and her pal Cinderella."

"Hello!" Anna rushed over to join us.

"Hi," I said.

We all three looked at Erin.

"Hi," she said, very quiet.

"The rumors are true," said Anna. "You do look very cute in your bridesmaid dress."

Erin smiled a little.

"We just tried on ours really quick to make sure they fit," said Anna.

"We're not even sure how we look in them," said Julia, "but who cares!"

The notebook was still opened to their NOT WICKED page. Without thinking, I wrote: *Not mirror-starers.*

"They're so long, we're afraid we're going to trip," said Anna.

"I'm afraid I'm going to trip too," said Erin. I was glad she was finally talking regular.

"We'll have to make a sister pact to catch each other if we fall," said Anna.

Erin laughed. "Okay."

"What's that?" asked Julia, looking at the notebook.

My face got very hot. "Um," I said.

Julia turned her head for a better look. "Are those our names?"

"Um." My face got even hotter.

"Are you writing about us?" Julia asked.

"Um." My face got the hottest ever. I looked at Erin.

Erin looked back at me and then took a very big breath and spilled the beans. "Yes, we are," she said.

My mouth popped open.

"What have you been writing?" asked Anna.

"We've been figuring out if you're wicked or not." Erin reached out and took the notebook.

My mouth stayed open, and now Anna's popped open too.

Julia smiled really big. "Why?"

"Because I didn't want to have wicked stepsisters," said Erin.

Julia laughed very loud.

"So, are you?" asked Erin, not sounding nervous or anything.

"I don't think so," said Anna, "but how would we know for sure?"

"We'll have to write down your information on pages in Cinderella's *WICKED STEPSISTERS NOTEBOOK*," said Erin. She held it up in front of her like she was giving a book report in school.

"Is that how you got your name?" asked Anna. "Do you have wicked stepsisters?"

My face was so scorchy now that my ears hurt.

"She just has one regular sister," said Erin. "But she did research on wicked stepsisters and then she made this notebook. See, it has a page for FOR-SURE WICKED and a page for NOT WICKED and a page for POSSIBLY WICKED."

Anna and Julia looked very interested.

"So, ready for some questions?" Erin asked.

"Yes!" Julia and Anna said.

"Do you have big feet?" Erin asked.

"I do," said Julia, "but Anna doesn't."

Erin turned to the FOR-SURE WICKED page and wrote: *Julia has big feet.* She turned to the NOT WICKED page and wrote: *Anna doesn't have big feet.*

"Are you loud and bossy?" Erin asked.

"I'm a little bossy," said Anna, "being the big sister and all."

Erin turned to the FOR-SURE WICKED page and wrote: *Anna is bossy.*

"And I'M LOUD!" shouted Julia.

Everyone in the kitchen stopped what they were doing and looked over at us.

"I'M LOUD TOO!" shouted Erin.

Julia gave Erin a high five.

"Can I see the *WICKED STEPSISTERS NOTEBOOK*?" Anna asked.

"Sure!" Erin handed it over.

Anna flipped through the notebook and then stopped. "Julia, look at this!"

Julia read the page Anna had stopped on. "Uh-oh," she said.

"Uh-oh is right," said Anna.

"What?" asked Erin.

Anna held up the FOR-SURE WICKED page and pointed to Erin's name. "It looks like we have to worry about you too."

"Oh yeah," said Erin. "I just figured . . . ," and she seemed like she didn't really know what to say.

"She just figured the more the merrier!" I said.

"I'm going to like having you for a little sis," said Anna.

"I already like it," said Julia.

Anna and Julia just couldn't get enough of that *WICKED STEPSISTERS NOTEBOOK*.

They asked a billion questions about it and laughed a ton. At first I was embarrassed, but Erin didn't care, so pretty soon I didn't care either.

The wedding went just fine except for when Julia almost fell. She really does have big feet, and she tripped over them coming down the stairs. Erin was right in front of her and Anna was right behind her, and they both put out their arms and saved her. She didn't even care that she almost fell in front of all those people. She laughed and said how lucky she was to have sisters around like Erin and Anna. And since Julia has a pretty loud voice, everyone heard and started saying that they agreed. The wedding stopped for a few minutes and then picked up again where it had left off.

For some reason the minister skipped over that wedding-stopping place. He could probably just tell that everyone was very, extremely happy and no one would object. When he finished up and the ceremony was over, the wedding got even more fun.

People in black walked around offering us food and napkins. There was champagne for the grown-ups and sparkling cider for the kids. Loud music played, and people started dancing. Erin told Anna and Julia all about how I was going to be the star of the Pumpkin Blossom Fairy dance, and they made me show them how to do it. Then they showed us how to do the hustle and the electric slide. We kicked off our shoes to do the moonwalk, which maybe wasn't very smart for me because I lost one of my wedges. I'm not too worried about it, though. It has my name and address on it, and it's somewhere in Erin's house. After they get the huge mess from the wedding cleaned up, I bet they'll find it.

My dad picked me up at 10 p.m., which was very late, but the reception was still going on. I told him all about everything, even the *WICKED STEP-SISTERS NOTEBOOK*. He wanted to see it, but I couldn't show it to him on account of Erin and Julia and Anna were giving it to their parents as a wedding gift. It seemed like a weird present to me, but Anna said it was just the perfect thing. She's planning on being a librarian when she grows up, so she probably knows.

15

Ballet Slippers

"I bet Miss Akiyama is going to be very mad when she finds out you haven't found your shoe yet," said Rosemary T. on the way to rehearsal. She slipped off the backseat, almost all the way to the floor, and slid her feet under the driver's seat.

"How do you know I haven't found it yet?" I asked.

She shrugged her shoulders. "I have some bad news."

"What is it?" I asked.

"I've looked everywhere for my old pair of tap

shoes, and I can't find them."

"Oh," I said.

"I must have lost them."

"You never lose anything," I said.

Rosemary T. said, "But I really did lose them!"

"Oh, honey, of course you did," said Mrs. Taylor. "We're so very sorry, Cinderella."

And then a big explosion went off in my head, and I closed my eyes tight. I didn't want Rosemary T. to know what was going on inside me, but this was it: I was in the middle of TROUBLE OF EPIC PROPORTIONS! All in capitals! It was two weeks until the Autumn Recital. I still hadn't found my missing tap shoe, and now I didn't have any to borrow.

"Here you are, girls," Mrs. Taylor said all cheerful. "Have a good practice. I'll pick you up afterward."

Rosemary T. unbuckled her seat belt and slid her feet even farther under the front seat.

It made it very, extremely difficult for me to get out, but I finally climbed over her and out the door.

I headed into the dance studio, and right there was Miss Akiyama. *Alas.* I took a big, deep breath and walked over to her; but before I could say anything, Rosemary T. raced over in front of me.

"Excuse me, Miss Akiyama," she said. "I was thinking that I should do the Pumpkin Blossom Fairy part today since Cinderella still hasn't found her shoe."

"You haven't?" Miss Akiyama asked me.

I shook my head and felt sad and horrible.

"With the recital coming up, someone else needs to practice the part," said Rosemary T.

Miss Akiyama sighed. "Fine. Switch parts, girls.

Cinderella, you can be a Dancing Pumpkin, and Rosemary can be the Pumpkin Blossom Fairy."

Then I got mad too! I was so mad, I wanted to yell and stamp my feet. I wanted to bonk Rosemary T. on the head with the Pumpkin Blossom Fairy wand very hard with a capital *H-A-R-D*. I also got a big lump of sad in my throat and I needed it to go away right away, because there was no way I was going to cry right there. I started tapping with my right foot and tried very hard not to blow my top, which means not to do all those things I just said.

Rosemary T. smiled. "I promise to be the best Pumpkin Blossom Fairy ever."

"It's just in case, Rosemary," said Miss Akiyama. "I'm sure Cinderella will find her shoe before our last rehearsal next week."

"Yes, I will!" I yelled, sort of blowing my top after all. Even though I couldn't think how that would be possible. And then I tapped out the Pumpkin Blossom Fairy solo right then as hard as I could stamp to make sure I didn't cry one bit.

Miss Akiyama laughed very loud, and everyone stared at her and me and Rosemary T.

I did not want to turn into a Dancing Pumpkin when Rosemary T. tapped me, and I did not think

I could make myself at all; but I did somehow or other.

When dance class was over, I stomped out to the car very fast and left Rosemary T. in the dust. I got in and sat down behind the driver's seat and buckled the seat belt and crossed my arms. When Rosemary T. got to the car, she said, "Move over." But I wouldn't budge.

"Move!" she said.

"No," I said.

Rosemary T. got very, extremely mad and put her hands on her hips and stamped her feet.

"I said, move out of my seat!" she yelled.

I pretended I couldn't hear her.

"THAT IS MY FAVORITE SEAT!" Rosemary T. screamed. "AND I SAID TO MOVE!"

"That's enough, Rosemary," said Mrs. Taylor. "Cinderella's already buckled in. Take the other seat, please."

Rosemary T. climbed in over me like I had to do to her earlier. She sat in the other seat and gave me mean stink eyes, but I just ignored her.

Mrs. Taylor started driving home, and the car was all quiet and very weird feeling.

"When did you decide that the seat behind me was your favorite, Rosemary?" asked Mrs. Taylor. "I thought you liked the one behind the passenger seat better because it was easier to see the video screen from there."

"No," said Rosemary T. very grumpy. "You're wrong because . . ."

But we'll never know why Mrs. Taylor was wrong because we turned the corner onto our street then and things were all wild and crazy and out of control.

Ralph was racing down the sidewalk with a Barbie doll in his mouth. Charlie was chasing right behind him, bouncing his basketball and yelling Ralph's name. Next came Mr. Hansen, who was yelling at Ralph too, and then Mrs. Hansen. She wasn't chasing Ralph, though; she was chasing her granddaughter, Jenny, who must have escaped too.

Just then Charlie made a grab for Ralph. His basketball flew in one direction and Ralph ran into the street. Mrs. Taylor had to screech on her brakes

so she didn't hit Ralph. We all went whooshing forward, and thank goodness for seat belts because we all went whooshing back where we belonged. And when I whooshed back, I felt a little thump of something sliding out from under the driver's seat and hitting my foot. I looked down, and there was my ruby red tap shoe!

"Are you okay, girls?" Mrs. Taylor was all out of breath and scared sounding. She pulled over to the curb right then and there and parked the car.

"Yes!" I yelled. I scooped up my tap shoe and held on to it for dear life. Even though we were way at the other end of the block, I jumped out of the car to find out about all the wild craziness.

"Thank you!" I yelled, and ran after Charlie.

When I caught up with everyone, they were on their way back to the Hansens'. Charlie was carrying Ralph and Ralph was carrying Barbie and Mr. Hansen was carrying Jenny and Mrs. Hansen was carrying Charlie's basketball.

"What'cha got there, Tinder?" called Charlie.

"What'cha got there, Tarles?" I called back, feeling proud that I thought of that.

"I've got an escape artist dog," he said.

"I've got my lost tap shoe!" I held the gate open,

and we all walked into the Hansens' yard.

Ralph was panting so hard from his long run that he dropped Barbie out of his mouth.

Jenny raced over and grabbed up her doll.

"Did she survive her adventure?" Mrs. Hansen asked.

Jenny turned her over and took a good, close look. "Yes!"

"That dog is going to be the end of me," Mr. Hansen muttered, and headed into the house.

"Where was your shoe?" Charlie asked.

"Underneath Rosemary T.'s front seat," I said.

"*Where?*" asked Charlie.

"Under . . . ," I started to say, but

then I had an *AHA!* I'd been so happy to find my shoe and so curious about the craziness on my block that I hadn't thought about anything else. But now I did. I looked down the block at Rosemary T.'s house with the meanest stink eyes ever.

"I will definitely be able to tell her never mind from now on," I said.

"I think you should be able to tell her more than that," said Charlie.

"I'm too happy," I said, and ran home to tell everyone my very, extremely exciting and wonderful-with-a-capital-*W* news.

We had to take two cars to the recital, which is not very green, but we had too many people for just one. My dad drove my Grandmother Smith and my Grandma B.; and my mom drove me and Tess and Erin, who we picked up on the way. Erin had decided to take dance class instead of basketball for the winter, and now I could introduce her to Miss Akiyama.

I walked into the dressing room clapping my tap shoes together, which is against the rules; but I was so excited I couldn't help it.

For the Pumpkin Blossom Dance, everyone had on

big, balloony pumpkin costumes except me. I had a tutu all full of different fallish colors like orange and brown and gold and red.

I also had a crown pinned onto my head and orange bows pinned on my shoes and the wand that I mentioned earlier.

In my humble opinion, which is something you say right before you say something good about yourself so you don't sound all braggy, the Pumpkin Blossom Dance was a bang-up success. We got a standing ovation, which Tess and Erin started; but standing ovations are contagious, and everyone caught it and stood up too.

Grandmother Smith and Grandma B. said I did a brilliant job and took tons of pictures. Erin said she couldn't wait to start taking dance classes, and Tess said "Bravo!" over and over again. That's a fancy way to say "Good job!" and I'm not sure where she learned it.

To celebrate we went out for ice cream afterward. I guess everyone else had the same idea too, because that place was chock-full of Pumpkins and Leaves and Acorns and Apples.

"I can tell what everyone else is, but what are you

supposed to be?" said a voice behind me. A basketball started bouncing. *Alas.*

I did a big, huge sigh and turned around. "What are you doing here?"

"We just won our basketball game and we're celebrating. How about you?"

"We just finished our dance recital and we're celebrating too," I said.

"Great," said Charlie. "So, what are you?"

"She's the Pumpkin Blossom Fairy." Erin handed me a scoop of chocolate mint. "She was great."

My cheeks warmed up a little.

Tess twirled up to us holding my wand and an ice-cream cone.

"Hey, watch that wand," said Charlie. "Don't turn me into a frog!"

"Frog, frog, frog!" yelled Tess, pointing at him with the wand.

"Help!" yelled Charlie.

Rosemary T. and Rosemary W. were walking by. "You're so loud," they said.

Erin and I gave them mean stink eyes.

"You better watch out," said Charlie. "Tess is turning people into frogs."

Tess whirled to them and raised her wand. "Fro . . . ," she started to say, but the Rosemarys backed away.

"That's enough, Tess." My dad scooped her up. "Ready to hit the road?"

"Sure." Erin and I followed my dad out. I turned around to say good-bye to Charlie, but he was off getting ice cream.

When we got home after dropping Erin off, one

of my ballet slippers was missing, but my mom didn't even raise her eyebrow. She and my dad and my grandmas got a great big laugh out of it on account of it being a slipper. You know, a *slipper*, like that other Cinderella. I did not think it was funny, though.

"This is very, extremely serious," I said. "I do not want to tell Miss Akiyama about another lost shoe. She might not let me take dance class anymore, and Erin's about to start."

Just then there was a crazy *knock-bounce-knock* at the front door.

"What in the world is that?" asked my Grandmother Smith.

"It must be Charlie," I said.

I opened the door, but there was no one there. "That's weird."

"Woilà!" said Tess, pointing with the fairy wand.

And there, sitting on the doormat, was my ballet slipper.

In between tripping over abandoned shoes, chasing after escaped pets, and searching for lost belongings,

Stephanie Barden

wrote this, her first book. She teaches classes at Woodland Park Zoo in Seattle, where she lives with her husband, Tom, son, Joe, and eighty-pound lapdog, Otis. You can visit her online at www.stephaniebarden.com.

Sherry Loeser

Photograph by Diane Goode

Diane Goode was born in Brooklyn, New York, and has a BA in fine arts from Queens College. Her distinguished list of picture books begins with the Caldecott Honor winner WHEN I WAS YOUNG IN THE MOUNTAINS by Cynthia Rylant. She lives and works in Watchung, New Jersey, with her husband, David, and their two dogs, Jack and Daisy. You can visit her online at www.dianegoode.com..